A TRUE UNICORN TALE

"THE JOURNEY TO UNICORNIA"

by Nannette Simone Furman

Illustrations by Robert Shilstone

Printed in the United States of America

ISBN-13: 978-1726775526

10 9 8 7 6 5 4 3 2

EMPIRE PUBLISHING

www.empirebookpublishing.com

ACKNOWLEDGEMENTS

For my three amazing unicorns, Jessica, Kristin and Gregory. Each of you shines with a unique, magical magnificence.

Thanks go to my amazing illustrator, Robbie Shilstone, whose talent knows no bounds. Especially exciting is the fact that he was my sixth grade student, quite a few years ago! My heartfelt thanks also go to my wonderful husband, and best friend, without whose patience and technical expertise this would not have been possible.

Thanks also go to Tiaga/Cristin B., a fabulously gifted yoga teacher, whose inspirational energy sparked this journey.

Thanks also go to Tina Z. for her expert editing help, and my dear friend, BettyAnn L. for her editing input.

This is a heartwarming story about a life-changing journey of friendship, self-discovery and acceptance, written for all budding unicorns who need to find and embrace their unique beauty, which is already inside them!

Table of Contents

Chapter One

The Problem

Once upon a time, there was a young, beautiful, perfect unicorn named Sasha. He did not feel perfect, but quite the opposite.

"Why am I so different?" he would cry to his mother. "All the other unicorns my age are smarter, have longer, brighter horns, can fly, and have friends. Added to that, I'm afraid of lizards and dragons!" (Which, as everyone knows, is very un-unicorn like)

"You're just a late bloomer dear," his mother lovingly responded. "You are unique and special just the way you are, and if you want a friend, you'll have to work harder at being a friend! Don't worry so much; you will blossom when the time is right, dear Sasha."

"Yeah, that works if you're a flower," grumbled Sasha, as he continued to feel and look different, crying himself to sleep every night.

His mother, worried, finally came up with the idea that she thought could help her son.

"I have arranged a meeting for you tomorrow. You will meet with Gurucorn, the wisest unicorn in our village. He will have some advice for you, my perfect son." Sasha, who was not amused, agreed. He felt he was far from perfect, because he was downright miserable, despite what his mom believed.

Chapter Two

Gurucorn, The Wise One

The next day, Sasha unexcitedly galloped off to the sacred Western Temple of the Unicorns to meet Gurucorn. It was noon, and the hot sun blazed in the sky like a fiery orange ball. Sasha's golden hooves glistened as his snow-white coat flashed brightly, contrasted by his flowing rainbow mane and long tail. His crystal blue eyes were framed by thick black eyelashes, a sight that captivated every unicorn. But all Sasha could see was "different," certainly not perfect, as his mother called him.

"Welcome Sasha!" greeted an old, yet handsomely attractive unicorn, standing in front of a beautiful white marble temple with four great columns. "I think I know why you are here," smiled The Wise One," but first I would like you to tell me in your own words."

Sasha, looking down, began to describe himself as being "defective and different." Gurucorn nodded, knowingly. "I see," he said, "let's walk a bit, as I have some very important things to tell you. I believe that what I am about to say will serve as useful tools to help you, as you venture on this challenging journey we call, LIFE," he continued, smiling warmly at Sasha.

"First, I want to tell you that you are, as are all of us, very special and unique. Be yourself! Trust in your intuition and let the universe show you the way. Your unicorn horn represents knowledge and wisdom. Everyone has this spot, right between and a bit above their two eyes-only yours is visible! When you focus on your goals, your THIRD EYE, as it's called, helps you follow your intuition, deep wisdom and spirituality. This helps you to discover the best path for you, and for your journey through life." Gurucorn stared deeply into Sasha's blue eyes as if he could see right into his thoughts.

Sasha shuddered, but then chuckled at the idea of having three eyes with one being a horn. He did not let Gurucorn see his smile and puzzled look as to the magical power of that middle one.

"The next tool," continued Gurucorn, enthusiastically, "is to learn to breathe in slowly, concentrating on pulling in positive energy and on visualizing or seeing good things. Then, slowly, with control, you must breathe out any negative thoughts or worries. You need to breathe this way three complete times. And when do you do this? You need to do this when you wake up, any time during the day, especially when you are tense or need to focus, and before you sleep. Practice this!" Gurucorn demanded loudly. "I know you're thinking that you already know how to breathe, but this is different. It is called a CLEANSING BREATH. It is breathing with control and purpose!" Gurucorn shouted again, with excitement, as he happily gestured to Sasha to try it.

Sasha tried three slow, controlled breaths. With each breath, he thought about breathing in positive energy, holding in his breath for a few moments, then releasing all tension as he blew out a long breath. "Wow!" he said, after completing three long breaths. "I feel so relaxed. I can do that to calm myself down and to help me focus? Pretty cool!" he happily exclaimed.

"My last bit of advice," smiled Gurucorn, "is that you go on a journey to the main unicorn temple, The Temple of Unicornia in the East. There, you will get your questions answered, as to why you are "different." Remember, life is a journey filled with many destinations, and this will be one of many!" And with that last remark, Gurucorn grinned and seemed to disappear, leaving Sasha stunned and speechless, but somehow, peacefully happy.

Sasha headed home, excited to tell his mother all about what he had learned.

That night, after explaining to his mother all the advice he'd gotten, Sasha went to bed and drifted into a deep, sweet sleep. He dreamed of Gurucorn, sipping from a golden goblet with sweet nectar, (ambrosia) as The Wise One, smilingly shared more advice to help Sasha with his quest.

"Sasha," he began, in a soft, soothing voice, "there are more things I wish to tell you. The first is that there are no such things as COINCIDENCES in life. Everything, every event, every being, every experience is put in your path for a reason. You must figure out why, so you can learn from each one. Just think about that for a moment! Use your third eye (horn-spot) to help you focus on your path. Next, be a good, kind, thoughtful unicorn who cares about others and try to make the world a better place. Do not judge others, but rather, try to understand them. Oh, and remember," he added, in a much louder voice," to practice controlled, purposeful breathing. Practice this at least three times daily!" he seemed to shout cheerfully.

Then... Poof!

And with that, Gurucorn was gone. "Did he disappear again?" thought Sasha. I'm in a dream, and this is not real. As he shook himself awake, he noticed a golden goblet on his night table.

Chapter Three

The Adventure Begins

After receiving motherly BE CAREFUL advice and saying goodbye to his mom, Sasha was off to find the Temple of Unicornia. It was a beautiful sunny day with a warm, jasmine scented, summer breeze blowing through the trees. Rays of bright sunlight pierced through the tall trees like cris-crossed beams of golden threads lighting his path. Leaves fluttered and danced across the path like a shower of red, and butter brown confetti. As Sasha approached the thickest part of the forest, the huge green trees seem to envelop him like a cool blanket, becoming heavier, dark and damp. Following the mysterious, quiet path, an eerie stillness and sudden fear came upon him. He found himself trying desperately not to think of dangerous dragons or low lurking lizards. As he remembered the wise words of Gurucorn, he started to breathe deeply and tried to relax, when suddenly, the silence was shattered by a high-pitched, piercing scream.

"Oh no!! Help, somebody!" came the desperate plea.

Sasha bolted toward the screams and suddenly came upon a clearing in the woods, revealing a raging, rushing river. There, in the not too far distance, he spotted what looked like a little green frog, with two suction-cupped hands, clinging onto a forked brown branch that was floating furiously down the rushing river. The frazzled frog frantically held on, screaming for help. Sasha knew he had

to do something. Taking a deep breath for strength, he galloped ahead of the floating frog and jumped into the middle of the river, just ahead of the frog, in an attempt to block its flight.

"Jump on my back!" screamed Sasha.

"I can't! You're too high! I'm afraid of heights!" frantically shouted the frazzled frog.

Sasha, thinking fast, lowered himself down into the rushing river rapids, securing his shiny golden hooves in the shallow sandy bottom. The little green frog approached, clinging on to the brown branch. As she floated by, her suction-cupped hands reluctantly released the branch, as she reached out and latched onto Sasha's floating tail. The abandoned branch barreled down the river, disappearing down an unseen, but very noisy waterfall just ahead.

Swimming ashore, Sasha climbed onto the sandy river bank with the frightened frog, desperately clinging to his tail.

"Thank you for saving me!" cried the frail frog, spitting out river water, gasping for air.

Chapter Four

A Froggy Friend

I'm just happy I was there! What a coincidence!" (Oops, thought Sasha, Gurucorn said that those do not exist. I will have to think about what this means later.)

"Well, let me introduce myself," said the pink-eyed, petite, green-bodied, big-handed frog. "My name is Fiona. I am very different from my species. I am afraid of heights and darkness. Some frog, eh?" she added, looking down sheepishly.

"I am also different, and I don't know why," responded Sasha. "I am a small unicorn, short-horned, can't fly, and I am also afraid of dragons and lizards! Some unicorn uh?" he added, sadly looking down at the sand.

They both looked dismayed until Sasha suddenly perked up and began telling Fiona about his quest, to go to The Temple of Unicornia to get his questions answered.

"Want to come? It's an adventure!" added Sasha, joyfully.

"Oh," thought Fiona for a brief moment. "Okay! And I can help you through the forest, as long as it's not too dark, and I don't have to climb too high," she added, rolling her eyes with an embarrassed look.

"Okay! So, climb onto my back. No wait, I'll lower myself down," said Sasha. Fiona scampered up his leg, across his back, and hopped towards his head. There, she nestled in nervously, but comfortably, attaching herself to Sasha's beautifully thick, rainbow mane.

They traveled until the cool crisp evening crept up silently upon them, covering the black velvet sky with a blanket of diamonds. They found a soft spot of brown leaves to rest on, and soon fell fast asleep, surrounded by the sweet scents of sage, lavender, and lilies.

Chapter Five

Choosing Challenge

As the golden sun arose like a bright brass ball in the cloudless blue sky, birds cheerily chirped, and rabbits roamed, happily hopping over clumps of clover, as the woods came alive with the chatter of animals. The pair awakened, were hungry, and happily found a perfect breakfast of blueberries and bugs.

"Onward with our adventure!" screamed Fiona, who cautiously hopped up onto Sasha, latching onto his mane, bravely trying not to look down.

Following a winding purple pansy-lined path, they suddenly heard the sweetest sound of a songbird singing, echoing through the woods. Sasha galloped towards the enchanting sound and came upon a beautiful bluebird, perched on a slate gray rock, centered in the middle of a crystal blue pond. The sun was shining on the bird like a golden spotlight, while the sparkling water rippled like a thousand happy dancing diamonds. As Sasha and Fiona approached in awe, something seemed to be slowly rising from the sparkling water near the rock. It was a huge, green, scaly, spike-tailed lizard, who suddenly shot out of the pond, at lightning speed to snatch the unsuspecting bird from its perch. The beautiful song suddenly stopped, and there was stone cold, dead silence.

"Oh no!" screamed Fiona. "Sasha! You have to do something!"

"Just breathe in positive energy, breathe out fear, and forget my loathing of lizards," chanted Sasha to himself several times.

"Okay! Hold on Fiona!" he shouted.

With that, Sasha leaped up and suddenly sprouted his wispy wings, flew to the middle of the pond, and pounced on the lizard's spine! This made the lizard choke and uncontrollably cough, thereby causing him to spit out the bluebird, who, at first, fearfully flapped, but then gracefully flew straight over the sparkling waters, past the edge of the pond to safety.

"Thank you, brave unicorn! You saved my life!" called back the beautiful bluebird as she flew into the woods. Sasha, flying to the other side of the pond, bowed, feeling both proud and totally shocked at his accomplishments.

"Whew!" sighed Sasha, taking a long, deep breath of relief.

"That was awesome!" screamed Fiona, jumping up and down. "I thought you couldn't fly and that you loathed lizards!"

"I couldn't fly, and I do loathe lizards!" responded Sasha, in self-amazement.

"And your horn! Oh my! It got longer and brighter! It's so beautiful!" shouted Fiona happily.

"No way! Really? I must be using my third eye, my intuition!" responded Sasha, with a sense of achievement.

"Well, whatever you're using, it's working. And you'll just have to trust me on this one since you can't see your own horn," giggled Fiona.

“Wow, what a day," sighed a smiling Sasha.

"Yeah, that's for sure," agreed a nodding Fiona.

Chapter Six

Annie in the Cave

Chatting and winding their way through a dark, damp, leafy green forest, the small path narrowed and abruptly ended at the mouth of a huge, green ivy and moss covered cave.

"Uh oh," exclaimed Fiona, eyeing the opening of the pitch black, dank cave. "Not good!"

"I know it's scary, but we have to go this way. It's the only path," said Sasha, in a determined voice.

"No way! No way! Not doing darkness!" screamed a fearful Fiona, hopping up and down." I'm already clinging to life, on your back with the height thing!" she added, tearing up, wanting to be brave yet truthful.

"Okay Fiona, I get it, but then we can't go forward and will never get to the temple to have our questions answered. Can we please just try it? I promise we'll go back if it's too much!" he added, feeling her panic as if it were his own. There was no response from the frightened Fiona.

Suddenly, the silence was broken when they heard a distant, small, but very powerful voice shouting. It was echoing from inside the dark cave.

"I'm done! I've had enough! I don't need anybody or anything!" the voice shouted.

Carefully watching the cave opening, waiting for something or someone to come out, they waited, and waited, and waited.

Then, it finally came out.

Sasha and Fiona were speechless.

"You must be kidding! That little thing made all of that noise?" giggled Fiona, who was now clinging to Sasha's ear. Blinking in disbelief, Sasha shook his head, smiling, nearly knocking Fiona off.

"Whatcha think ya all looking at?" belted out a small red ant, who was standing up, shaking her little fist. "Never saw a red ant who could stand and shout? Well, apparently neither has anyone else around here, so I'm outta this cave!" She waited for a response, but Sasha and Fiona were wide-eyed, stunned, and silent.

"Hello! I'm Annie, by the way, if anyone cares," she added sarcastically while stretching her neck and staring up at Sasha with outstretched hands.

Sasha and a giggling Fiona remained speechless.

"Cat got your tongue? Don't even think about another giggle greenie! And you-what's that thing coming out of your head?" She snapped, pointing at Sasha's glowing horn.

Fiona and Sasha suddenly burst out laughing. Annie shook her head, smiled, and looked pleased with herself, instantly liking the two.

“Well,” started Sasha, breathing with purpose and trying to think about why they came upon a very unique ant with unusual characteristics.

“We're on a journey to the Temple of Unicornia, to get answers to our questions,” he explained.

“And do I want to know what those might be?” inquired Annie sharply.

“Well, we were wondering why,” began Fiona, “we're so different from our kind, or species."

“Who cares?" snapped Annie. "Just get used to the nasty looks, the mean names, all the laughter, and the loneliness. I've had enough, and decided to leave it all behind, actually today," sniffed the standing ant. “I am very different! I stand, I talk (actually shout), and I am red, not black like the rest of my kind. I shouldn't even be an ant! I am alone in the world, but that's okay!” bitterly belted out Annie, clearly holding back tears.

“Well, you don't have to be alone,” said Sasha, feeling his heart would break if he didn't help Annie. “Come with us, Annie, please! Be part of our quest!”

“Please come!” piped up Fiona, enthusiastically hopping up and down, carefully clutching Sasha's mane.

Annie looked down and thought for a moment. Then she responded, "Okay. I can probably even help us to get through the crystal caves because I know them.”

“Sounds great! Climb up!” responded Sasha, excited that Annie agreed to join them on their journey.

So, Annie scampered up Sasha's leg, onto his back, and up his rainbow mane. The ant was graciously greeted by

Fiona's froggy green hand that pulled her up, right next to her. The three were underway, following a path that neatly narrowed, leading them into a gloomy, cold, mossy-green ivy covered cave.

Chapter Seven

Crystal Cavern

Okay guys, stop here. I have some good and bad news about the Crystal Cave," started Annie, rather loudly, which sent shivers up Fiona's froggy spine.

"What we need to do to get through this cave is to follow the multi-colored crystal stones in the walls. I will stand up and scout for you, ("good thing" mumbled Fiona) so we can stay on the rather dim path. That's the good news," continued Annie. "The bad news is that we will have to get past hundreds of big black bats, and... the ferociously fierce, famous dragon named, Flagon."

"Oh no!" groaned Fiona and Sasha. "No amount of breathing can help me with this one!" added Sasha, as he began his cleansing breaths, thinking, BREATHE IN BRAVERY, AND OUT, FEAR!

And so, the three unlikely companions ventured off into the cold, crystal cave, each battling their own fears. Sasha was petrified of dragons and lizards. Fiona was scared of heights and the dark, and Annie had to curb her shouting, as dragons do not like unexpected noises because it uncontrollably sets off their fire-breathing.

The cave smelled mildly muddy, musty, and was very dusky and dank. As soon as they entered, Fiona efficiently pointed out, as they noticed, the small rays of hopeful spots of light peeking through the cave's rough, rocky ceiling. This fabulous feature let the beautiful multi-colored crystals shine like scattered stars, lighting up the dark path with tiny jewel-like lights. As Sasha picked his way through the uneven rocky path, Fiona clung to his mane, while Annie shouted directions, trying to whisper. All three quietly shook with fear at every scary step, as the silence was deafening.

Suddenly, seemingly out of nowhere, they heard vibrating sounds, then whoosh, flap, whoosh! Sasha's view of the path was blocked by black things flying everywhere! It was like a swarm of big black bugs with gauze capes, darting, and whizzing in front of them. Fear paralyzed the three, as Annie screamed out very loudly,

"Just stand still! They will stop!!"

Fiona shut one eye, focusing the other on a beautiful pattern of blue wall crystals, beaming out a shred of hope in the cold, creepy blackness. Annie kept watch as Sasha began to deep breathe with purpose-in positive-out negative.

Chapter Eight

Dreaded Dragon

Quiet finally came. All flapping and noises came to a dead, silent stop. The adventurers felt a cool, crisp breeze flowing through the cave, followed by the unexpected appearance of a beautiful, shining soft white glow that seemed to light up the path ahead.

"Wow! So cool!" said Annie and Fiona in unison.

It was like a golden glowing saber, lighting the path. Only, it was actually, Sasha's horn! Sasha began to feel and now actually see, that his breathing, focus, and intuition was working! This began to make him feel much more self-confident and ready, he thought, to face the next challenge, which, by the way, came all too soon.

Just as they began to feel relaxed, they felt the cool air change into a toasty breeze of intense heat, followed by the sight of what looked like a wall up ahead, of red-yellow flames.

"Oh no!" screamed Annie. "It's all my fault! I spoke too loudly, and we all know what that means!"

"Not just you, we all did," piped up Sasha and Fiona in defense.

And there IT was... Flames, shooting out of a tiny three-foot Dragon!

"What?" shouted Annie. "That's it? That thing is the dreaded dragon Flagon? Ha! You must be kidding!"

“Stand back or I will reduce you to cinders!” shrieked the tiny blue dragon in a shaky, unimpressive voice.

“Who’s he kidding? He couldn’t roast marshmallows with that flame!” snapped Annie, throwing her hands up in disbelief.

“We don’t know that for sure,” whispered Fiona, shaking her head side to side.

Feeling confident with his improved horn, Sasha, sensing the danger was minimal, stepped slowly forward, approaching Flagon with a soft voice, filled with compassion.

Chapter Nine

One More Member

"Hi, Flagon! That is you, isn't it? We've heard so much about you, and have not come to harm you. We only wish to pass through this cave to get to the Temple of Unicornia."

"What do you mean we? I only see you," said Flagon, questioningly.

"Oh! I have two friends with me, in my mane. Come on you two! Show yourselves!" Reluctantly but bravely, the two stood up and waved to the small blue dragon, who shyly nodded.

"Well, I will not, and actually cannot stop you. I am an orphan and a dwarf dragon who can't control my fire-breathing and cannot fly. I am truly a dragon-dud, and do not know why I am so different from all the other dragons," sniffed Flagon, as tears began to flow, forming puddles at the dwarf dragon's feet. The three would have laughed at the,

"Why am I so different?" question, but the sight of Flagon in tears, reduced them all to sympathetic sniffles.

“Then you really need to come with us,” said Sasha in a confidently commanding voice, "because we ALL have the same question we'd like an answer to."

“Oh definitely!” piped up the other two. Flagon looked around, in momentary thought, smiled and nodded a shy yes, feeling wanted, for the first time in his little lonely life.

Chapter Ten

Challenging Changes

As their chatter-filled journey days went by, the foursome discussed their lives, their likes, their fears and anything that came to mind. Together, they began to realize that although they were very different, they were also similar in many ways, some very good ways.

Sasha began to trust his intuition, (third eye) to follow his path. He had (once at least) faced his fear of lizards, was traveling with a (although tiny) dragon, and he actually flew! Several times daily, he practiced his breathing- in positive energy and out negative, and he was beginning to feel self-confident and calm, ready to embrace the next challenge-that he knew would surely come.

As for Fiona the frog, fears of heights and darkness had lessened. Not that she rushed into dark caves or hopped up to high heights, but she felt that maybe she could do both things if she had to.

Annie, the ant, began to see her ability to speak as an actual asset, but she now needed to work on the shouting part. Being able to stand made her a great look-out on Sasha's back. As for being red, "I'm just going to have to deal with it; I cannot change that, but I can change how I deal with it!" she thought.

Flagon, the dwarf dragon, still felt like a dim-dragon because he could not fly yet, and was working, constantly, on controlling his fire-breathing. He had occasional uncontrollable bursts, which resulted in his reducing several tall trees to smoldering cinders. But at least he hadn't fried his three friends yet; he consoled himself.

They all felt that there was much to discover, as Sasha told them that Gurucorn had said, "Life is a journey," and now they could each follow their own journey, but with friends!

Chapter Eleven

A Confusing Crossroad

As the four followed the footpath-sized road, it suddenly divided into two choices, with no sign in sight for the temple.

"I don't know which way to go!" stammered Sasha, starting to hold his breath, an old habit. "Just breathe," he told himself repeatedly, eyes darting left-right-left-right.

"I say go to the left," said Fiona, "because it's much brighter than that right hand, darker road."

"If I could fly, I'd check out both, but I can't," piped up Flagon, sadly feeling useless.

"Just wait a minute!" screamed Annie so loudly, that everyone was startled. "I am really trying to control that, sorry," she added. "Hey! What's that?"

"Well good day, noble unicorn!" a sing-song voice echoed from up high in the tall trees. The four gaped in amazement at the sheer beauty of the beautiful bluebird and her sweet song. "May I be of help, as you once helped me?"

she asked, in a sing-song voice that left the foursome breathless in awe.

"Hello, beautiful bird!" responded an eager Sasha. "Great to see and hear you!" he added passionately. "We are wondering which path to choose. Can you help?" implored Sasha, beginning to think that there really was no hope for them to accurately decide which way to go.

"Maybe I can help, as I do have an idea," chirped the bird, beautifully singing every word.

"Whoa! Cool! Who is that?" belched out Flagon, with a shot of flames that nearly fried the beautiful bluebird, who frantically flapped, flew higher up, freeing herself from the sudden burst of ferocious flames.

"Oops! So, so sorry!" whispered Flagon. "I'm so working on that!" he added bashfully.

"That's okay!" sang the bluebird. "I've gotten a lot faster since my lizard experience!"

They all laughed, except Flagon, who had no idea what they were laughing about. So he smiled.

"Although I, myself, do not actually know which way to go, I do have some advice. You need to focus, concentrate, and ask the universe to give you the intuition to know which path to take. You all have an invisible third eye to tap into, even though Sasha's is visible." They all giggled at this. "This is the area of intuition, deep wisdom, and spirituality. This will lead you on toward your true path. Trust that you will all get the right information from your focusing, and the universe will help you so that you will choose the correct path for each of you!"

"Okay, thank you," replied Sasha. "We will all work on our individual and group concentration abilities. We will use the tool of breathing in and out, with awareness, to collectively find which way is best for us. That's great advice!

Thank you!" Sasha then nodded to the other three who shook their heads in agreement.

“Well, good luck!” sang the bluebird as she swiftly soared up and away into the beautiful blue and pink cloudless summer sky.

“Okay, guys! Let’s close our eyes, concentrate, breathe in and out deeply, and focus on our third eye!” At that moment, Sasha’s beautiful golden horn lengthened and glowed like a saber of hope and white light.

“Wow!” shouted Annie. “I mean-that’s amazing!” She added in a much quieter voice, wondering how she'd look with a horn that glowed but shaking off the idea as wild.

“Let’s do it now,” piped up Fiona, "I'm so ready!"

“Okay, but I just hope that all this deep breathing doesn’t set off my fire-blasting skills! I think I will face the other way just in case,” added Flagon with a grin.

They all became quiet, (which was not easy for Annie) closed their eyes, and focused on which path to take. They concentrated on breathing deeply, to keep themselves focused, which lasted almost two very long minutes.

"Okay," said Sasha. "Are we ready to share?" he asked, as his head began to turn towards the towering tall green trees framing the right fork in the road. His unicorn horn glowed white, shining like a saber in the sun. Simultaneously, the three others, with closed eyes, pointed in the exact same direction! As the sun was setting in the west and sinking in the sky like a gold coin melting, they all had pointed to the road going east.

“Wow! So cool! It worked!” shouted Flagon, gulping in a hot breath of smoke, nearly choking with excitement. They all chuckled with delight and satisfaction.

Chapter Twelve

Forging Forward

So for four hours, the foursome picked their way through the tall tree-lined, multi-colored pebble-paved path, as the silent silver moon smiled, sending out moonbeams that lit up the ground stones like jewels. A cool calm steady wind washed over the four adventurers, as they cheerily chatted, each exchanging more personal stories of their past, some painful, some sweet.

"Just because we are different from our own kind, maybe isn't such a bad thing, as we each have unique traits that do come in handy," said Sasha to himself. He was experiencing much more self-confidence in his ability to trust in his intuition, as he had flown, and faced his lizard and (small) dragon fears! Not that his fears were gone, but they were somewhat diminished, which made him feel empowered.

Fiona thought about how she had dealt with darkness, and felt that she was beginning to overcome her other fear, heights. She was still working on both, but feeling much more self-assured.

Annie was beginning to appreciate her weird-ant ability to stand, as she made a great lookout guide. Controlling her shouting, (as ants don't even talk) was a work in progress, she thought. As for her red color, "I'm beginning to feel good about that! I'm seeing myself as rocking the red look," she told Fiona, who laughed, loving Annie's sassy attitude.

Flagon, still feeling like a dim-dragon was still undeniably small, blue, couldn't control his fire-breathing and still feared flying. He saw those last two skills as his next challenge, which presented itself so much sooner than he would have liked.

Chapter Thirteen

Dreaded Dragonia

After a few more days of talkative traveling, the four friends forged their way closer towards the Temple of Unicornia. Then suddenly, seemingly out of nowhere, came a huge roaring sound, followed by a big blast of red-orange flames up ahead. The tall tree-lined path ahead turned into a wall of smoke and cinders.

When the smoke cleared, there appeared a horribly huge purple dragon, with fiery red-yellow eyes, and a tremendous twitching tail that toppled trees in its path as it slapped from side to side.

"I am the Dreaded Dragon Dragonia!" bellowed the menacing monster with an aura of mystical madness.

"Ohhh no," mumbled Fiona and Annie in unison.

"No one ever crosses this path!" she howled, holding her ground with a deadly demonic determination.

They all looked at each other with wide eyes and thunder- pounding hearts.

Sasha took a deep breath, and in split-second thought, he immediately turned to Flagon, who was right behind him.

"Hey! I have an idea! I will fly to the right of Dragonia, distracting her. You go left and run as fast as you can. She should be distracted by me so that you can slip past her, but we've got to do it fast and now! We will meet up a little way down that path, hopefully way past Dragonia."

Flagon nodded in nervous agreement.

"Hold on Annie and Fiona, and make a lot of noise, start screaming!" shouted Sasha. And without a moment's hesitation, racing forward, he fearlessly headed forward and noisily flew up and over the unsuspecting, startled, fire-breathing Dragonia, clearing well past the dragon. Landing way up ahead, he looked back to see where Flagon was. They were horrified at what they saw.

Dragonia furiously shot out more red fire flames, but had just missed Sasha. She seethed and steamed with aggressive anger.

Hissing, over missing Sasha, Dragonia now set her red-yellow eyes on the very frightened tiny blue dragon, Flagon, who had been left in the path, directly in front of her. He was so immobilized by fear that he forgot to move when Sasha flew!!

Stunned, but as if suddenly awakened, Flagon shouted, "Here I go!" And the feisty little Flagon charged right at the dreaded dragon, fearlessly firing his flames into a rhythmic breath-of-fire that blasted Dragonia's nose, stuffing her nostrils with blasts of suffocating smoke. He bravely barreled up her face, sent more smoldering blasts up her nostrils and then suddenly- took flight! The blast of his flames caused so much smoke that the choking Dragonia, staggered, blinded by teary eyes, lost her balance, flopped backward and landed on the ground with a thunderous thud that could be heard for miles.

Flagon sailed forward over the rest of the dizzy Dragonia, following the tall tree path until he caught up with his friends, gracefully circling over them.

"No way!" screamed Annie, jumping up and down, more like a grasshopper than an ant.

"Look at you, up there!" pointed Fiona with her froggy green suction cup finger.

"Yikes! You were amazing, and you're flying!" shouted Sasha, as Flagon carefully landed beside him.

"I thought I was a dead dragon," confessed Flagon. "It worked! I worked! I flew!" added the elated dragon.

"You were spectacular!" screamed Annie.

"Yes you were!" agreed Fiona with a giggle.

"Great flying Flagon! We all did it!! Great teamwork!!" added Sasha with excitement and relief.

Annie and Fiona climbed off of Sasha for a group hug, that kind of hug that warms your heart, and makes a memory you know you will never forget.

Chapter Fourteen

The Temple of Unicornia

After a well-deserved sweet slumber, nestled in lavender leaves, the adventurers continued onward, sensing that they were very near the Temple of Unicornia, and indeed they were.

They came upon a clearing, the next morning, as the narrow tree-lined path opened like a golden gate into a beautiful meadow of emerald green grass, studded with bursts of pink and blue tulips. Enchanted by the magical meadow, they almost missed the small, shiny silver sign that read, "The Temple of Unicornia Welcomes You, Spiritual Travelers." The foursome looked at each other with wide eyes and exhilaration that they each had never before experienced.

Once they crossed over a small hill, they saw it. The Temple of Unicornia, straight ahead. The poplar trees neatly lined the road like huge green lollipops, paving the long path to what looked like a tremendous temple with twenty great white marble pillars, surrounded by wispy weeping willows, flowing in the breeze, framing the path like a river around the temple. The foursome was speechless at the sheer beauty and the feeling of tranquility (quiet and calm) that came over them as they approached the sacred temple. The path ended with a small series of white marble steps which led to the entrance of the Temple of Unicornia.

The adventurers mounted the steps, which led them to a seven-tier marble fountain, flowing with sun-drenched sparkling blue water. On each level of the fountain was a golden plaque with a letter and an explanation for each letter. This is what they saw:

T= trust in the universe to guide us
E= energy needed for good deeds
M= mindfulness in everything we do
P= peace for all living things
L= love for yourself and for others
E= enthusiasm for your journey – life

"Wow! This place is awesome!" whispered Annie.

"There's a lot to think about," added Fiona.

"I feel like there is so much to learn here, but I don't even know where to start," said Sasha with an excited yet perplexed look.

"Well, I think we should just ask someone who may know how we can get our questions answered. I still want to know why I'm so different," added Flagon, actually wondering if that really mattered anymore.

Almost instantly, a beautifully handsome, silver-haired unicorn appeared.

"Hello! I am Cosmicorn, and I couldn't help overhearing your conversation. I hope you don't mind, but I believe I can help you if you would like me to," said the unicorn with the bearing of a kind king.

"Oh yes! That would be most kind of you, and appreciated by all of us, I believe," said Sasha, glancing towards his friends who readily nodded in agreement.

"Well you, no doubt, were sent by a WISE ONE who gave you lots of advice. We call that advice, "The Tools of Life," stated Cosmicorn with a knowing smile.

"Oh yes! That's very true!" responded Sasha.

"Well then, let me first ask you this. How was your journey?" asked Cosmicorn, glancing around at the foursome, but stopping at Sasha.

"Oh my! It was totally amazing! It was very scary, challenging, and fun. I met new friends and learned so much about myself that I do not know where to start," beamed Sasha as his horn again glowed golden like a sacred saber.

"And so," continued Cosmicorn, who warmly and wisely looked at the other three, "do you all share similar feelings?"

"Oh yes, definitely!" they chimed in unison.

"Well, that is what you were all meant to do! You went on a journey, learned a lot about each other and yourselves. It's all about your journey, not just the destination!" he chuckled, waving towards the fountain.

They all smiled, in thought, and nodded.

"Now, all you need to do is to read and think about the words on the fountain. Then, you will need to spend some time walking around our, GROWTH GARDEN, gathering the tools you will need for your return journey. Please do stay a few days, so each of you can reflect on your own individual journey, as this is very important to your personal progress."

And with that, Cosmicorn bowed and seemed to disappear, leaving Sasha thinking, again? Why is it that they give you great advice and then poof! They're gone!

So the foursome followed the path to the Growth Garden, which was lined with fragrant lilies, red roses, and wispy weeping willows that gently brushed against their cheeks as they followed the garden's path, pausing to read each of the ten silver signs.

<u>Here is what the ten signs said:</u>

1. Be yourself, you are unique and have a special purpose.
2. You have your own power within you, find it.
3. Don't judge others-understand them.
4. Celebrate the differences in all beings and in life.
5. Remember to breathe in positive energy, and out negative energy, or anything that does not serve you well.
6. Use your third eye, the seat of your intuition, wisdom, and spirituality.
7. Trust that the universe will guide your journey.
8. Everything and everyone has been put in your path for a reason. Find out what you are meant to learn to go forward.
9. There is no such thing as a coincidence.
10. Want a friend, be a friend; treat others exactly the way you would like to be treated.

Chapter Fifteen

The Destination

As the adventurers meandered through the Growth Garden, they felt as if they were floating through a magical maze, filled with the sweet scents of fragrant flowers and the beautiful sight of wonderful, wispy, weeping willows. Each sign they came upon was carefully carved with shiny silver letters that sparkled like the moon on a blanket of black velvet. The foursome could hear faint sounds of chimes, dancing in the warm, sweetly scented summer breeze. As they followed the fragrant, flower-petal paved path, they each began to reflect upon the journey that took them to the temple, as each sign had a message that seemed to ring like a beautiful bell.

Each silver sign was surrounded by a crystal blue pond with sparkling waters that glittered like happy, dancing diamonds.

As they walked along the path, each of the four friends found themselves in deep thought, thinking about their own adventure, the journey that led them right here, where it seems they were meant to be.

"Let's stop here," said Fiona. Annie agreed, as Sasha lowered himself down, so the two could hop off.

"I'm going to go on," said Flagon, "because this place is amazing!" he added, lost in his own thoughts.

"Just go where you want, we'll catch up later," said Annie, who was mesmerized by the sign that read:" Be yourself, you are unique and have a special purpose."

Fiona, while gazing at the sparkly diamonds dancing on the pond, began to reflect on her rather fragile froggy past. She had a family of three other siblings, two brothers and one sister, who was mean to her. They called her names, telling her that she was a failure as a frog and a disgrace to the entire frog family because she was afraid of heights and darkness. Her sister, Fredonia called her Fat-Handed Freaky Fiona. She wasn't even sure her family loved her as she always felt ignored, and began to spend more time by herself.

That's how Fiona ended up one day, sulking and resting on a tree branch just above the relaxing rushing waters of a raging river. The branch had snapped, and she floated uncontrollably down the river when Sasha dove in for the rescue!

"Wow! What a lucky save!" she thought. "That situation started a whole chain of events that led me here! Oh... Sasha said that there is a reason for everything... there is no such thing as a coincidence! Wow! He is right! I found friends, and I've gone through so many experiences that have helped me feel stronger, and not like a freaky frog failure! I am so much more okay with being different than I was. Wow! And learning to tap into my own third eye for wisdom, and breathe in positive energy are two tools I have gotten from Sasha that have really helped me to become stronger."

Annie was drawn in by the sign that read: "Be yourself, you are unique and have a special purpose." This made her think of her nickname, "Reject Annie Ant." She was red, could stand and speak, even shout! These were not ant-like characteristics, and so Annie was bullied in school and at home. As she thought about the word "unique," she began to review the journey with fresh eyes, realizing that her "differences" actually made her unique, and an asset to Sasha and her friends. Also, learning to breathe deeply when stressed, helped her to control her voice volume, so that was a really helpful skill she'd learned. As for her red color, she decided it was exotic, and she would embrace it. "I'm really okay being me!"

Flagon had gone ahead, stopping at the silver sign that glowed, "You have the power within you. Find it." This made sense to him as he began to reflect on all the adventures he'd had, and he began to realize how much he felt like a changed dragon. He had fought his fear of Dragonia, used his fire-breathing with more control, and best of all, he focused on his third eye, his intuition and actually flew!

Flagon knew he had a lot more work to do to become an effectively feared dragon, but for now, he felt more powerful and was thrilled to have friends. "Maybe being feared isn't so important," he said to himself. "Working on myself, my skills, and being a good friend may just be enough!"

As Sasha strolled along the path, he began to feel that each silver sign really meant something important to him and his journey. "I am so different from that depressed unicorn who cried himself to sleep every night! I had no friends, no self-confidence, and a small dull horn. I couldn't fly, and I was afraid of lizards and dragons! Look at me now! One of my best friends IS a dragon! (Okay, not a huge one, but he is a dragon!) Sasha was drawn to one silver sign in particular, probably because Gurucorn and Cosmicorn had spoken of this: "Everything and everyone has been put in your path for a reason. Find out what you are meant to learn to go forward."

Reflecting on his journey, Sasha came to the realization that every event, every individual, whether seemingly bad or good held a purpose. "I have been tested, challenged, and called upon to use my third eye to concentrate. Breathing in positive energy, and out, any fears also helped to calm me down. I can see that if I use the advice given to me by the elder unicorns and the Growth Garden, it's like I have the magic tools for every journey I will go on! And, I also made some fabulous friends along the way!" he shouted aloud, feeling like Annie in her uncontrollable moments.

After a few days, Sasha called his three friends together to see if they were ready to leave The Temple of Unicornia.

"What do you think? Are you three ready to head home and embark on some new adventures on the way?" he asked, with a sly smile, sparkly blue eyes, and thick long lashes that he had come to appreciate as unicorn unique and cool! along with his glowing golden horn.

"Oh yes!" shouted Fiona and Annie in unity.

"Well, I don't really have a home to go back to.." stammered Flagon, belching out tiny puffs of smoke.

"Actually, neither do we!" belted out Fiona and Annie, looking at each other with sad wide eyes.

"Great! So it's settled!" responded Sasha with confidence. "It's back home to my home, which will be our home. My mom will love you guys! You are my friends! She will be so happy to have a bigger family!" he added with a giggle, horn glowing.

"Yeah, like she's really going to want to adopt a feisty red ant, a fearless frog, and determined dragon?" piped up Annie sarcastically, with a partial smile.

"Oh, you don't know my mom! She'll love you three!" responded Sasha with such clear confidence that no one dared disagree.

So, they found Cosmicorn, who thanked them for visiting and wished them well on their journey, after giving them a size-appropriate scroll of the temple fountain words and the "Ten Tools."

"Remember, all four of you: Read the fountain words and the tools scroll; breathe, and use your third eye, your intuition, for wisdom. Go forth and follow your heart, it will always be your best guide!" he added, as he seemed to disappear suddenly.

Poof!

"Did you see that?" questioned Sasha. But the threesome was too busy gathering their tools to notice.

And so, the four unlikely friends set off together, armed with their tools, for their next adventure, to add more experiences to the journey called "life."

The End!

About the Author

Nannette Simone Furman

Nannette Simone Furman is a recently retired Bedford, NY middle school English teacher, who has a tutoring practice, is a Reiki Master, and a Kundalini yoga teacher. She has three fabulous grown children and an adorable grandson. Nannette lives with her wonderful husband and a beautiful Brittany spaniel, Ginger, in Las Vegas, Nevada. They enjoy hikes in Mt. Charleston, exercising and spending time with family in California.

The Illustrator

Robbie Shilstone

Robbie Shilstone has always had an overactive imagination. While growing up in the outskirts of New York City, Robbie was exposed to the beautiful nature in the surrounding area as well as the cultured areas in the city. Whether for illustration or animation, his work has always encapsulated character, humor, and his passion for nature. After graduating from University, he has been working on his children's book promoting peace and a love for the earth we live on. You can find more of his work at: www.shilstonearts.com

Made in the USA
Middletown, DE
17 February 2021